THE ADVENTURES OF
JOSHUA
AND
PIP
CALVIN THE CATFISH

This book is dedicated to my Mama for all the love and encouragement she has shown me my entire life. And for giving me the freedom to live, play, and explore my world.
-J.L.,Jr.

For Lily- Never stop chasing the big ones and don't eat all of the taffy.- J.R.G

ISBN: 978-1-7347263-3-6

Summary: On a humidly hot day, Joshua and Pip are geared up and ready for a great day of fishing. On the way to Ogeechee Lake, they see a sign that challenges them to catch Calvin the Catfish. Pip is ready and willing to accept the challenge. However, Pip and Joshua soon find out that catching any fish, let alone the great CALVIN THE CATFISH, takes lots of patience and a little luck.

THE ADVENTURES OF
JOSHUA
AND
PIP
CALVIN THE CATFISH

Words by
John Light Jr.

Pictures by
Jamie R. Gandy

Once upon a time,
on a humidly hot day,
Pip and Joshua met
on Oak Tree Hill.

Pip held two fishing rods. Joshua carried a bucket and a can of worms. They were going to Ogeechee Lake to fish.

As they walked up Greentown Road, they passed a sign that read: "Will You Catch Calvin the Catfish?"

Pip's eyes widened. "I'm gonna catch Calvin!" he exclaimed.

Joshua reasoned, "I just want to catch a fish."

WILL YOU CATCH
CALVIN
THE
CATFISH?

When they arrived, the lake was crowded. It seemed like the whole town was there.

They heard two old men talking close by.

"I know I felt my line jump. I almost had him. I know it!" exclaimed the man in the brown jacket.

"Oh man, you didn't feel a thing except your belly growling. I'm the one that almost caught Calvin!"

They continued to argue, "Besides, you didn't bring the salt water taffy like I told you. Everyone knows you need taffy to lure Calvin!"

Pip turned to Joshua," Do we have any taffy?"

"No we have worms." Joshua said.

"Gummy worms?" Pip hoped.

"No, wormy worms." Joshua explained. "But, I do have some cherry bubble gum."

"That will have to do." Pip decided.

The boys found an empty spot on the lake. They baited their lines. Joshua used worms. Pip used bubble gum.

They casted their lines and then they waited. And
waited. And waited some more.

They heard a shout. Three sisters each pulled a brown bass out of the lake.

Then, there was another celebration. A teenage boy caught four flapping crappies at once!

But Pip and Joshua had not caught anything.
The boys continued to wait.

An hour passed. The sisters packed up their fish and went home.

Another hour passed. The teenager took off. He was happy with his haul. The boys continued to wait.

Finally, the sun began to rest its eyes in the western sky. The once crowded lake was now empty. Only Pip and Joshua were left.

Joshua asked," Are you ready to go? It's getting dark."

Just as Pip was about to reel in his line something snatched at it! Pip held on as tight as he could.

"Help! I got something Joshua!" Pip pleaded.

Joshua grabbed Pip. The line pulled them to the left and then the right.

Then, the line pulled them forward. They pulled backwards.

Suddenly, a great big monster of a fish leapt out of the lake! Pip and Joshua were astonished. It was Calvin the Catfish! It seemed to wink and smile as it soared through the sky. Then, it plunged back into the Ogeechee.

Water splashed everywhere. They were drenched. They lost their fishing rods, but there were fish all around them.

They collected the fish. "No one is ever going to believe we saw Calvin the Catfish!" Pip proclaimed.

"I know!" Joshua agreed. "But I will never forget the look on Calvin's face!" Joshua mimicked.

Pip and Joshua laughed as they walked home down Greentown Road.

That is the end of this Joshua and Pip adventure.

CPSIA information can be obtained
at www.ICGtesting.com
Printed in the USA
LVHW070551020721
691728LV00003B/77